You Want My Dog
To Get A Job?

ALSO IN THE POSITIVE BOOKS FOR POSITIVE KIDS SERIES

Millie's Lost Adventure

Chloe, Where Are You?

Lauren's Angel

Lindsey and The Christmas Puppy

Millie Meets Bugger

Second Grade Spelling Challenge

Radar And The Time Capsule Mystery

A Puppy Fashion Show

Kitten Trouble

Maddie Moves Away

Lindsey Goes To The Dentist

Larry And The Christmas Cat

Lacey's Cupcake Battle

You Want My Dog To Get A Job?

Lindsey And The Lost Baby Bird

Why Do I Have To Say Thank You?

Princess Lauren And Her Magic Wand

Daisy The Foster Puppy

Bella's Secret

Sally The Stray Puppy

You Want My Dog to Get a Job?

Written by Lynn Marie Lusch

Edited by Randi Marie Gause

CONTENTS

HOMEWORK

"I want to give you a special assignment, but I need your help," Mrs. Browning announced to the class.

"You're asking US what we want to do for homework?" Jeff asked, with a very surprised look on his face.

"Not exactly," Mrs. Browning answered, smiling.

My name is Lindsey Marie Robbins. I'm seven years old and in Mrs. Browning's second grade class at Bay View Elementary School, in California. It's Friday afternoon and our teacher is giving the class a project for homework.

"I want everyone to write a story, but I need help with the subject of the story," she continued. "I really want you to use your imagination."

"Can I imagine I already got an A, and don't have to write anything?" Brett asked. He always gets into trouble with his sassy remarks.

"Nice try," Mrs. Browning replied. She leaned against her desk and began explaining, "Every one of you has a very vivid imagination. I hear different things you say about all kinds of subjects, and I think it is wonderful! Now I want you to write it down."

"I don't understand," Andrea said, with a very worried look on her face.

"This is what I was thinking," Mrs. Browning explained. "Everyone in here loves animals, how you care for our class's hamsters, Millie and Maggie, is proof. I would like you to write a story about your pet. Maybe have them talk, or play a game with you. I want them to come to life, more than just being an animal."

"Like, do you want my cat to do chores?" Madison wondered.

"Or play video games?" Trent added.

"Do you want my dog to get a job?" Steve asked.

"Yes! That's it!" Mrs. Browning exclaimed, looking at Steve. She looked very excited.

"What exactly are we writing about?" I asked. Melissa looked at me and I could tell she was totally confused, also.

"I want you to write a story about your pet, and what kind of job they would have, if animals had jobs. I want you to imagine they go to work, just like your mom or dad. They get up in the morning, get dressed, and go to their job. I want to know what they do, and where they work," Mrs. Browning explained.

"I don't have a pet," Michael stated.

"What kind would you like to have?" Mrs. Browning asked. "Let's make this more interesting.

It doesn't have to be a pet you have, but one you would love to have. For example," she explained, "let's say you have a cat, but always wanted a dog. Or a horse. Or an eagle! How about a pet alligator? Or a dolphin."

"Oh I get it!" Michael stated. "I can pretend I have a pet gorilla. You want me to figure out what kind of job he would have, and write a story about it."

"Exactly!" Mrs. Browning exclaimed. "So, Michael's friendly pet gorilla would be in charge of setting up swings in all the playgrounds and schools around town. He also sells bananas as a snack."

Everyone giggled thinking about a gorilla going from playground to playground, testing out the swings, and then working at a banana stand.

"My dog is a poodle," Jeff began, "she's my mom's. I like her and all, and I play with her in the house, but her name is Fifi. My mom polishes her toe nails and puts pink ribbons in her hair. A guy like me can't exactly take a dressed-up dog like that for a walk around the neighborhood. It would ruin my reputation!" All the boys agreed with Jeff. "So I can pretend I have a bulldog? And write a story about him?" He asked.

"Yes!" Mrs. Browning answered. "But make sure he's nice to Fifi," she smiled.

"I will," Jeff grinned. "This is gonna be good!"

"Any more questions?" Mrs. Browning asked the class. No one raised their hand. "That is your assignment, and you have all weekend to work on it.

Papers will be turned in Monday, and each one of you will read it in front of the class on Monday afternoon. Have fun with this, and use your imagination! Anything is possible!"

CHLOE? OR LULU?

Melissa is my very best friend. We live in the same neighborhood and ride the bus to and from school together every day!

"So which puppy are you gonna write about? Chloe or Lulu?" Melissa asked me as we sat together on the bus.

"I'm not sure," I answered. "I guess I have to think about it for a while and figure out which dog would have an interesting job."

Chloe and Lulu are my two fluffy puppies. Chloe is all black, and has a white spot on her chin and her chest. Lulu is pure white and a little bit smaller. I love them both so much, and I have written stories about them for homework, but not a story like this.

"Are you going to write about Twinkles?" I asked Melissa.

Twinkles was Melissa's cat, well she kind of still is, but doesn't live with her. When the cat lived at Melissa's house, her mom found out Melissa's little brother, Derek, is allergic to furry animals, so they had to give Twinkles away. Luckily, her Aunt Becky has a cat named Smoke, because he's all gray, and she happily took Twinkles to be Smoke's friend. Melissa gets to visit Twinkles every time she goes to her Aunt Becky's house.

"Definitely!" Melissa said, eagerly. "So, what kind of job do you think a real come-to-life, cat would have?"

"Hmmm," I answered, "this is going to be interesting." Melissa nodded her head up and down in agreement.

CHLOE, CAR SALES PUPPY

I got off the bus with my big sister, Lacey, and we started walking down the street to our home. Lacey is in sixth grade, and she's eleven years old. She has lots of good ideas, and I think I'm going to have to ask everyone for ideas for this project.

"So Lacey, what kind of job do you think Chloe would have if she was a person?" I asked.

"Chloe and a job? Wow Lindsey, this is a fun homework project," she responded, smiling. "You can create just about anything!"

"Well I could, but I really want to think about this one. If Chloe got up in the morning, got dressed, drank coffee," Lacey was giggling thinking about this, "got in her car," Lacey was laughing now, "and drove to work, where would she go?"

"One question?" Lacey asked. "What kind of car would she drive?"

Now I was laughing! "Chloe would probably like a convertible, so her face would always be in the wind!"

"Then she would be a car salesman, or saleswoman, or salesdog, whatever! So she would look forward to going to work everyday to enjoy the wind. But she would have to get a haircut so she didn't worry about how her hair looked!"

Lacey and I were laughing like crazy as we walked in the front door of our house.

"School must have been fun today!" Mom said when we walked into the kitchen, still laughing. Mom was making dinner, macaroni and cheese, oh yum! My little sister, Lauren, was playing, I don't exactly know what. She was walking around carrying books, and was still in her pre-school clothes, but had her two fairy headbands in her hair. She's three years old, and has the best imagination I have ever seen!

"Lauren, why are you wearing two tiaras in your hair?" I asked, confused.

"Because I'm a pretty pretty princess!" She answered, very matter of factly. She kept walking around the kitchen as if she were in charge of something.

"Lindsey has the best homework ever!" Lacey told Mom.

"What is it?" Mom asked.

"I get to decide what kind of job Chloe or Lulu would have, if they had jobs," I sort of explained to Mom.

"Oh now that is fun!" Mom exclaimed. "Let's see, Chloe is more of a free spirit, so she would have a fun job. Lulu is bossy, and doesn't realize how little she is, so she would be more serious."

"Chloe sells cars," Lacey told Mom. "We already decided that. She specializes in convertibles and sports cars," Lacey started laughing again.

"Lulu," I said, thoughtfully. "What would she do?"

Just then Chloe and Lulu came running in the kitchen, Lulu yapped at us, then ran back out.

"Yep, she's serious," Lacey said, looking at Lulu chasing Chloe around the house. Everyone burst out laughing.

SATURDAY MORNING

Saturday morning Melissa came over to my house to play. We also thought we would discuss the homework project.

"Have you thought any more about which puppy you are going to write about?" Melissa asked me. We decided to take the puppies for a walk to the park. Melissa held Chloe's leash, I had Lulu's.

"Lacey and I decided that Chloe would be a car sales, ahh, person, I guess," I told her. "She loves the wind in her face, so we figured she would specialize in convertibles and sports cars."

Melissa giggled. "I could see that! She would have commercials on TV saying, 'Come down to Chloe's Puppy Lot this Sunday for a special deal.'"

I started laughing, "But for some reason I think I want to write about Lulu. Still trying to figure out what she would do." I was making a squished-up face.

"Twinkles has me a little confused," Melissa explained. "I have to write about something with her eyes."

"You do!" I answered. "Out of all the cats I've ever seen, Twinkles' eyes really do twinkle. They have to do something magic!"

"Ooohhh magic! That's it!" Melissa exclaimed.

We got to the middle of the park and took the puppies off their leashes. Melissa and I each had a small bag of tiny treats, and we stood far apart from each other. We took turns calling the puppies, and when they would run across to us after we called their names, we gave them a treat as a reward.

After about ten minutes we hooked the pups back on their leashes and headed toward home.

When we got back to my house, we went into the kitchen so the puppies could get a drink of water, and Melissa and I could get a glass of fruit punch. Lauren came marching into the kitchen, still wearing two tiaras, and announced that she needed Lulu to help her with her homework.

"What kind of homework do you have?" Melissa asked Lauren.

"It's important," Lauren answered very seriously. "Lulu is my teacher, and I'm her special student, so she gets to help me with my letters. Come on Lulu," Lauren headed out of the kitchen with both puppies following her.

"Lulu, a teacher, hmmm," I said, looking at Melissa.

"I would make sure I was in school every day if Lulu was my teacher," Melissa said, giggling.

"That gives me an idea," I said, smiling.

"Lindsey, if it's ok, I think I'm going to go home and write down some ideas for my story," Melissa said, eagerly.

"I think I'm going to go work on this, too," I answered. "For some reason I have all these ideas floating around my head. I better write some down and get started!"

I walked Melissa to the front door and watched her jump on her bike and ride home. Then I went upstairs to Lauren's room, to watch the teacher.

Lauren was sitting on the floor facing her bed. Chloe was lying down next to her, completely not interested in school. Lulu was at the edge of Lauren's bed, sitting, looking down at Lauren.

"Now this is the letter L," Lauren said to Lulu, and held up her magnetic letter L. "This is A, this is a U, this is an R, this is E, this is an N," Lauren said to Lulu as she held each letter up, and then put them next to each other on the floor. "This spells Lauren, that's my name," Lauren said proudly. Lulu yapped and wagged her tail.

"Does that mean you did good?" I asked Lauren.

"Yes it does," Lauren said proudly. "Miss Lulu always yaps and wags her tail when I do good work. Sometimes she licks me."

"What does she do if you make a mistake?" I wondered.

"She barks at you! Not real loud, just a little, so you know you need to fix it," Lauren explained, with a very serious look on her face.

"I get it," I answered. "I'm going to do some of

my own homework, keep up the good work, Lauren," I said as I walked to my room. I had so many ideas swirling in my head, I couldn't wait to write them down!

I sat at my desk and took out a piece of notebook paper. At the top I wrote, "Lulu the Pre-School Teacher," then I began writing.

"Lulu is a pre-school teacher for three year olds at Bay View Pre-School. Her favorite subject to teach is spelling, so she teaches the alphabet. Miss Lulu wants everyone to know how to spell their name."

Hmm, this is good, I thought to myself. I decided this is going to be my topic. What else would she do if she were a teacher? I had so many ideas, I started writing really fast!

LET THE STORIES BEGIN

In school Monday morning everyone was talking about the project. No one minded doing homework over the weekend, I think everyone had too much fun!

Mrs. Browning collected all the stories. She said she was going to read them during lunch, then we would all take turns reading them out loud. The whole class couldn't wait until lunchtime!

When the lunch bell rang everyone went as quickly as they could to the cafeteria. We all ate our lunches and then went back to our classroom before the bell rang. Mrs. Browning looked up from her desk when we all started walking in.

"Well, either the cafeteria served liver for lunch, or everyone wants to hear stories," she smiled at us.

"Stories!" Everyone said at once.

LULU THE PRE-SCHOOL TEACHER

"Lindsey, why don't you go first," Mrs. Browning said to me, as she handed me my paper.

"Okay," I answered. I was actually excited about reading my story first.

"I have a pet puppy named Lulu. She is a pre-school teacher. Everyone in her class is three years old, and the students like that she is a little puppy. Miss Lulu's favorite subject to teach is spelling. She wants to be sure everyone learns all the letters, how to spell and how to read."

I looked up at the class and everyone was paying attention. I loved this!

"Lulu sits on her desk and looks over all her students. The first thing she does is have each one learn how to spell their name. She has a big teacher's box full of magnetic letters. Everyone takes turns sitting in front of her. They are supposed to take each letter of their name out of the box, show it to Miss Lulu, and say what the letter is. Then they put it on the whiteboard and when they're done, it should spell their name."

I looked at Mrs. Browning and she was smiling at me. I wonder if she picked me first because I had a teacher story?

"If someone makes a mistake and picks up the wrong letter, Lulu yaps at them. Then they know it's wrong and they go back to the box and get another letter. If it's the right letter, Miss Lulu stands on her desk and wags her tail at them. If a student is really misbehaving, Miss Lulu jumps off the desk and barks really loud right in front of them. She keeps barking until they behave. They usually will behave quickly because for such a small dog, she has a really loud bark. Everyone loves Miss Lulu, and she is proud that the whole pre-school class knows how to spell their names."

I went back to my seat and looked over at Melissa. "That was really good!" She whispered, "I can see Lulu doing that!" She giggled.

JERRY THE BRONTOSAURUS

Brett stood in the front of the class with his paper.

"I have a pet Brontosaurus. His name is Jerry. He has a very special job in the gardening industry. He's a tree trimmer." Brett looked up from his paper at the class and grinned.

"Every Saturday morning I take Jerry around the neighborhood, because that's when he works. I ride on his back when we walk down the street. He stops in front of each house and I slide down his back to get off. He waits for me in the front yard as I go up to each house. I knock on the door and ask the people who live there if they would like to have their trees trimmed. If they say yes, I tell them we charge five dollars per tree, and ask them to show me which trees they want trimmed. Then I lead Jerry to each tree and point at it. Jerry starts eating the leaves from the top of that tree. Then they are trimmed."

Brett stopped and looked at Mrs. Browning. She was listening carefully and nodded her head for him to continue.

"Sometimes, we only will work on one street that day if there are a lot of trees to be trimmed. A brontosaurus can only eat so many leaves. If we get done early, Jerry lets the neighborhood kids climb on him and he takes them for a walk. He doesn't really run because he would make too much noise and scare people."

Everyone in the class was listening. A dinosaur as a pet! Wow!

Brett continued, "We don't charge the kids that take rides, that is free. When we are done, I climb back up on Jerry's back and we walk home. He lives in my back yard. You can see him from anywhere because he's taller than my house. But he is very friendly, that's why my mom lets me keep him. The End."

Brett grinned big and sat in his seat. All the boys were saying cool things to him, and I agreed. I would have never thought of that!

TWINKLES THE MAGIC CAT

It was Melissa's turn. She took her paper from Mrs. Browning and stood in front of the class.

"Twinkles is a magic cat. Her eyes sparkle so much that she can turn the lights on and off in our house. That is when I decided she needed a job. Twinkles is the one that turns the lights on in the whole town!" Melissa looked up at the class and giggled.

"Every evening, when it starts to get dark out, Twinkles walks up and down the streets. She stops at each light pole, looks up at it and blinks. The light automatically goes on! She does that on every street. She does this every night. Then in the morning, she walks the same streets and does it again to shut them off. This would seem like a lot of work for one cat, but she is very mysterious. Twinkles does this so easily that people can be walking down a street and have a light go on and they don't even see her. Cats are like that!"

All the girls in the class were nodding their heads

up and down, agreeing with Melissa.

"During the day, Twinkles mostly takes naps. But if it's a rainy or gloomy day, she will sneak out of the house to turn lights on. She doesn't want anyone to be afraid of the dark. During Christmas time, Twinkles has an extra job. People will put up their Christmas trees, and if they want the lights to twinkle, they call me. I take Twinkles over to their house and she looks at their tree and blinks. Then the tree lights twinkle! She only has to do this once, it will last the whole Christmas season."

Melissa looked up from her paper at the class and was smiling. I was too, this was a very good story!

"So please remember Twinkles's very special job, and be sure to call me during Christmas time. Thank you."

Everyone clapped and Melissa was smiling.

MAX THE POLICE OFFICER

It was Jeff's turn.

"I have a bulldog named Max," Jeff read from his paper. "One day, Fifi was walking down the street with my mom. They were walking together nicely, and Fifi felt especially pretty. My mom had just put polish on her toes and new bows in her hair. They were going to the store. A big, mean, stinky dog started following them and was making fun of Fifi. It made her feel bad. Max was walking across the street and saw Fifi being picked on, and went over to stick up for her. 'Leave her alone' Max said in his very deep voice to the mean dog. 'She didn't do anything to you, mind your own business and quit being mean.' His voice was so deep and he said it so firmly, the big, stinky dog turned around and they never saw him again."

Jeff looked up at the class to be sure everyone was paying attention. They were, and you could see that the girls were worried about Fifi.

"When my mom saw what Max did, she said, 'Oh

what a brave dog, do you have a home?'" Jeff was pretending he was talking like his mom, so he would switch voices from his mom to Max. He had everyone laughing, including Mrs. Browning.

"'No, I don't,' Max said deeply. 'Well, you must come home with us,' my mom told him. 'We will make sure you have a comfortable bed, and good food. You are a hero.' So Max followed my mom and Fifi back home, and he lives with us. But everyday he walks around the neighborhood making sure there are no mean dogs picking on fluffy dogs. He's the only dog police officer in Bay View, and he is very proud of it." Jeff looked up from his paper and grinned. Everyone clapped.

MICHAEL'S GORILLA

Before Michael started reading his paper, he looked at the class and said, "I really liked the idea Mrs. Browning gave me on Friday, about a gorilla, so that's what I wrote about."

He then began, "I have a pet gorilla. His name is Bob. Bob works for the schools and playground departments. Whenever a new school is being built, or a neighborhood is putting in a new park, they call Bob. They ask him how many swings they should have, and what other playground equipment they should put in. Bob knows all the neighborhoods and all the kids. He is able to tell them how many swings will be needed."

The way Michael was reading his paper reminded me of how my dad reads the newspaper, really serious.

He continued, "Bob is waiting at the playground when the new equipment arrives. He checks it and makes sure the guys install it properly. Then he sits on each swing and makes sure it swings high enough. When he thinks it does, he goes on to the next one. Bob likes to watch kids on swings, it makes him happy when kids are laughing and playing and having a good time. So you will see Bob going from playground to playground. If the kids are having a lot of fun, he gives each one a banana. That is Bob's favorite treat and he likes to share. So, if you see a big gorilla walking around with a bunch of bananas, don't be afraid, it's Bob. He's just doing his job making sure kids are having fun. Every town needs their own Bob."

I really like Michael's story. It seems like Bob has a very important job.

TONY THE TICKLER

Matthew was next.

"I have a pet monkey named Tony. Everyone calls him 'Tony the Tickler.' His job is to make people laugh when something sad happens."

Matthew looked up from his paper to see if people were paying attention. Everyone was sitting nicely with their hands folded on their desks. He continued when he was sure people were listening.

"Tony has an automatic built in alarm in his head, kind of like a robot. If someone falls when they're running, or gets hit with a baseball, he knows instantly where they are. He goes to them, listens to them when they tell him what happened, he makes sure they don't need an ambulance or anything, then he tickles them to make them laugh. Laughter is the best medicine. He doesn't tickle them so much that it hurts or makes them cry, he just wants them to laugh. Then, when Tony is sure they're ok, he moves on to help someone else."

Matthew took a deep breath, then kept reading.

"Once in awhile a doctor's office will send him a signal, or a hospital, and Tony goes there and the nurses will tell him who he has to help. But mostly, he just waits around for someone in the neighborhood. It doesn't matter how old you are, Tony wants you to know everything will be ok. The End."

"Matthew," Mrs. Browning asked, "where did you get the idea for Tony?"

"My grandpa," Matthew answered. He was still standing in the front of the classroom, "I kind of fall off my bike a lot."

"He sure does," said Jeff, rolling his eyes.

"And one time my grandpa was at our house when I walked, or limped, in with a scraped up knee. He listened to what happened, asked me if I need an ambulance, and I said, 'no Mom will clean my knee up.' He said everything was going to be ok, forget about it, and told me a funny story. Then he started to tickle me to make me laugh. He said, 'Laughter is the Best Medicine.' He said if something sad happens, something good will happen too, and forget about the sad thing. The fastest way to make something good happen is to be happy and think happy thoughts."

Everyone nodded their head up and down yes, agreeing with Matthew's grandpa.

"My grandpa's name is Tony, that's why I named my monkey Tony," Matthew said, as he sat back down in his seat.

"Well, I think your grandpa will be very happy when you read him this story," Mrs. Browning smiled at Matthew.

"Yeah, I think he will," Matthew smiled.

THE THREE AMIGOS

Mrs. Browning called Emily next.

"I have three dogs," Emily began. "They are Chihuahuas. Their names are Rose, Lilly, and Tulip. My dad calls them the three amigos. That means friends. My mom says they have so much energy she wishes they would help her clean our house. So this is their job, they clean houses."

"Ohhh," everyone said. "That makes sense," Andrea said, nodding.

Emily continued, "My dad made them business cards that say, 'The Three Amigos Cleaning Service, We Clean Houses Fast.' Each dog does a certain chore. Rose likes to drag things, so she jumps on each bed and pulls off, with her teeth, the dirty sheets. She drags them into the laundry room, jumps on the washer and shoves the dirty sheets in there. Then Rose goes into the linen closet and pulls clean sheets off the shelf. She drags them into the bedroom and jumps on the bed and straightens them out."

I was imagining a little Chihuahua changing sheets on a bed. It was kind of funny!

"Lilly's job," Emily continued, "is to put things away. She runs through the house and picks up toys on the floor and puts them in the toy box. She will put newspapers in recycling, and if there are books on the floor, she nudges them until they are in a nice, straight pile. If she finds clothes on the floor or thrown on a chair, she grabs them with her mouth and puts them in the closet. Then she checks all the rooms to make sure everything is neat."

Emily looked up from her paper and smiled at everyone, then told us about Tulip.

"Tulip is in charge of dusting the furniture. She has a fuzzy dust mop and carries it in her mouth. She jumps on the furniture and drags the dust mop across it. After each piece of furniture, she takes the mop outside through the doggy door, and when she's outside she shakes with it in her mouth. That cleans all the dust off. Then she goes back in the house and does the same thing to another piece of furniture. Tulip does this until the house is all clean with no dust."

Emily had a good story. She wasn't finished yet!

"Since my mom doesn't have to clean her house anymore, she works for the 'Three Amigos Cleaning Service.' She is the manager. She spends all day on the phone scheduling houses for the dogs. The dogs are very happy because they get to have fun and earn money. Every time they get paid, they go shopping and buy new squeaky toys and sweaters. Chihuahuas can never have too many sweaters or toys."

Emily sat back down in her seat.

"Emily, is it alright if I call your mom to schedule the cleaners for my house?" Mrs. Browning asked. Everyone started laughing.

JON THE PILOT

Chad was next.

"I have a pet German shepherd. He is giant size, like he weighs 150 pounds, and he is all black. He is a helicopter pilot, and his job is to make sure traffic runs smoothly."

Everyone was listening closely because it would be so cool to have a dog fly a helicopter!

"Every morning, everyone listens to the radio for Pilot Jon. They want to make sure they get to work on time. Pilot Jon flies over all the major highways. If someone has a flat tire and is holding up traffic, Jon gets on the radio and tells people to drive down a different street. Tow truck drivers also listen to him on the radio because then they will know where they can go to help someone and fix a car. This also gives them a job."

Chad looked at everyone and grinned.

"Pilot Jon also watches for people who speed, because speeding can cause an accident. If someone is going too fast, Pilot Jon will fly over that car and shine a bright light on it. This lets the driver know he better slow down. It also lets other drivers know there is someone driving carelessly when they see the bright beam in the sky. It's a red beam, so you can even see it during the day. Drivers are always embarrassed when the beam lands on their car because they know everyone around them knows they messed up and did something wrong, and Pilot Jon is sort of yelling at them. Jon believes this is the only time it is ok to embarrass someone. It is for the safety of everyone on the road."

Chad let out a deep breath, and continued, "Pilot Jon was awarded a medal by the President of the United States. I got to go with him to Washington D.C. This is the first time a dog has been awarded a medal by the President for safety. Pilot Jon has made our city the safest to drive in, in the whole United States."

Chad sat down and everyone clapped. A dog flying a helicopter. Cool!

KEVIN THE TURTLE

Mrs. Browning gave Brian his paper to read.

"My name is Brian and I have a pet turtle. His name is Kevin. He is a big turtle and walks on his hind legs. He wears glasses and works at the newspaper. He is a very good artist, and draws a comic strip for the paper everyday. The boss of the newspaper told Kevin they probably wouldn't sell any newspapers if it wasn't for his comic strip. It is that good and funny and popular."

Brian looked up at the class for a second, and then continued, "But every night Kevin has a secret. He comes home from work, eats his dinner, then he waits for it to start getting dark. He takes off his glasses and puts on a mask because he's NINJA TURTLE!"

All the boys in the class started clapping and yelling, they love ninja turtles! Brian made a ninja turtle pose in front of the class.

"Kevin walks the streets making sure the city is safe. He carries a big machine gun. If he sees someone robbing a store, or trying to hurt someone, he shoots them with his machine gun that shoots out silly string. It is a special silly string, and automatically wraps around the person. Then it dries into a hard plastic so the bad guy can't move."

Brian was enjoying reading his story.

"Kevin has to keep his identity a secret, so after the person is all wrapped up in string he calls the police and tells them where they are and what he caught them doing. The police come and take them to jail. The police want to give the ninja turtle an award for bravery, but they don't know who he is. They put posters on poles and in store windows asking for him to come to the police station so they can shake his hand and say thank you. Every time Kevin walks down a street and sees one of the posters, he just smiles. He has a secret."

Brian sat down and a couple of the boys patted him on the back because they liked his story so much.

CLYDE THE SCHOOL BUS DRIVER

Michelle stood in the front of the class with her paper.

"I have a pet horse. He's a Clydesdale and is very, very big. His job is taking children to school, so he is like the school's bus driver. But he doesn't drive a bus, he gives everyone a ride to school on his back."

All the girls said, "Ooooohhh." Melissa whispered to me, "How awesome would that be!"

"My horse's name is Timothy, but because he's a Clydesdale his nickname is Clyde. He's so big he gives six kids a ride at one time, even with their backpacks. I trained him to kneel down on his front legs. He does this so everyone can get on and off of him."

Michelle peeked up from her paper to see if people were listening, they were.

"Clyde goes up and down the street to each bus stop. If he has someone on his back and they are goofing around or being loud, he stops and tells them to behave. He doesn't want anyone to fall off of him. If they don't listen, when he gets to school he tells their teacher that they can no longer get a ride on him. This has only happened a couple times, no one wants to have Clyde say they can't ride him anymore."

"The school was awarded a trophy for having the best attendance out of every school in the city. The principal said it was because of Clyde. Everyone loves getting a ride to school on a horse."

Michelle sat down and Melissa said to her, "That would be so much fun!"

MORE AND MORE STORIES

Everyone had such good stories! Amanda wrote about a butterfly that was in charge of putting the colors in all the flowers.

Rachael wrote about her pet eagle. He flew around protecting all the other birds because he was so big and strong.

Lisa has a pet dolphin. He works at Bay View Recreation Center teaching everyone how to be good swimmers.

This was the best homework ever! I could tell everyone thought so. Everyone was very polite and listened to each story.

Finally, everyone had had their turn. Mrs. Browning walked up to the front of the class and sat at her desk.

"Children, you did an outstanding job! I can't pick the best story because there isn't one, they're all the best!" Everyone was smiling and agreeing with Mrs. Browning.

"Don't ever stop using your imagination. This is what will help you create, invent, or achieve just about anything. You can invent a new video game, solve a complicated problem, create an invention that will help people! Just think, if you can imagine Brett riding down the street on the back of a brontosaurus, anything is possible."

"You got that right," Brett said out loud, with a big grin.

This was the best homework I have ever had in my whole life! I think I'm going to keep writing stories, maybe one day I'll be an author!

ABOUT THE AUTHOR

I am the mother of two daughters and a faithful student of the "Positive Thinking" philosophy, as well as a believer in the "Law of Attraction." Unfortunately, it was not until I was in my thirties that I was introduced to, and began to take part in, these teachings. Fascinated with these studies, there was one question I would ask myself every time I was introduced to a new author or book on this topic – why wasn't I taught this as a child? If I had been, I wouldn't have developed some of the unhealthy attitudes and opinions that I worked for years to reverse.

My series of books contains subtle messages of positive thinking, as well as a reminder to always have a "don't give up" attitude on a child's level. The messages are entwined in mysteries or short stories that are entertaining for the child to read themselves, or for someone to read aloud. I hope you and your children enjoy them. Thank you.

Lynn Marie Lusch

Visit our website: www.kidspositivebooks.com for easy ordering and other notes of interest. You can also find our books directly on Amazon.

Parents, please visit us on Facebook to stay up to date on new releases and other exciting news: www.facebook.com/kidspositivebooks

Like our page and share your and your child's favorite part of the book!

Contact us at: Lynn@kidspositivebooks.com

Made in the USA
Middletown, DE
28 February 2024